MOO COW KABOOM!

Story and pictures by
THACHER HURD

For Carolyn North

Moo Cow Kaboom   Copyright © 2003 by Thacher Hurd   Printed in the U.S.A. All rights reserved.   www.harperchildrens.com

Library of Congress Cataloging-in-Publication Data is available.   ISBN 0-06-050501-X — ISBN 0-06-050502-8 (lib. bdg.)

1 2 3 4 5 6 7 8 9 10   ❖   First Edition

HarperCollins*Publishers*

It happened one night,
while Farmer George
and the pigs
and the chickens
were sound asleep.

The pigs fell over.
The chickens
jumped ten feet.
A rocket trail
blazed across the sky.

Farmer George ran outside in his nightshirt.
"Where's my Moo Cow?
Where's she got to now?"

Where his Moo Cow should have been
there was just a patch of burned grass.
Farmer George called the Sheriff.

The Sheriff arrived with his hounds.
"Where's my Moo Cow?" said Farmer George.
"Beats me," said the Sheriff.

The hounds just howled at the moon.
"Woe is me," said Farmer George.

Meanwhile . . .

Moo Cow was far away,
cownapped by a Space Cowboy
named Zork.
At a zillion miles an hour
they zoomed past Mars and Pluto,
over the Big Dipper,
and straight through the Milky Way.

The flying saucer landed
on Zork's farm,
in a galaxy far, far away.
The zigs on Zork's farm fell over
when they saw the strange
earthling creature.
The zickens jumped ten feet.

Welcome Aliens!
THE INTER-GALACTIC RODEO
For the first time ever! Zork the Cowboy (that's me) will ride THE WILD MOO COW from Planet Earth!
Lunk Wrestling

Zork jumped on Moo Cow's back.
"Giddyup!" yelled Zork.
Moo Cow didn't move.
"Git along, little dogie!" yelled Zork.
Moo Cow didn't move.

Zork swatted Moo Cow
with his hat and yelled,
"LAZY, USELESS,
UNCOOPERATIVE,
UNINTELLIGENT
EARTHLING MOO COW!"
Moo Cow didn't like that at all.

All of a sudden . . .

Moo Cow whirled.

Moo Cow twirled.

She danced.

She pranced.

Then she bounced
and boogied

and bucked so high that Zork
flew all the way back to his farm.
KABOOM!

"YIKES!" cried the aliens.
"This Wild Beast Earthling Moo Cow
is too wild for our rodeo!"
They put Moo Cow in a flying saucer
and blasted her back into space.

So long, Moo Cow!

Moo Cow pushed a button: **Beep Beep!**
Moo Cow pulled a lever: **Thunk!**
Then she bumped into the rocket switch:
SHA-ZOOM!!!
and blasted back through the Milky Way
at a zillion miles an hour.

Around and around and around
went the flying saucer.

Moo Cow turned slightly green.
But which way was home?
Moo Cow didn't know.

Then she saw . . .

. . . something she remembered.

And soon,
far below, there was
Farmer George's farm.
Just as the flying saucer
was about to crash,
Moo Cow bailed out.
 Down,
  down,
    down she floated . . .

Farmer George fell over.
The pigs fell over.
The chickens jumped ten feet.

"Well, I'll be," said Farmer George.

Moo Cow ate green grass.
Moo Cow chewed.
Moo Cow MOOOOOOOED...

happy to be an earthling Moo Cow,
home again on Farmer George's farm.